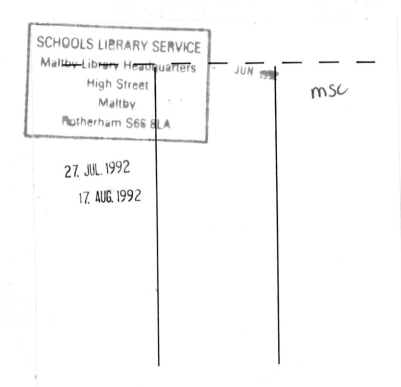

WESTWARD WITH
COLUMBUS

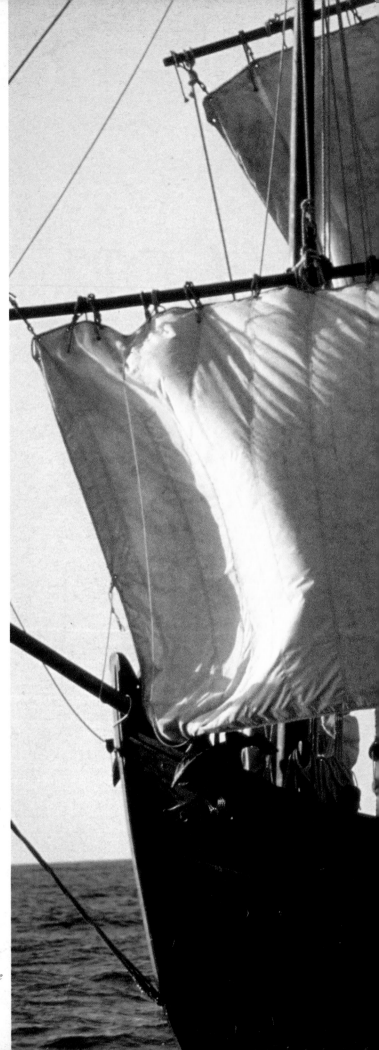

Design and compilation © 1991 The Madison Press Limited
Text © 1991 John Dyson
Photographs © 1991 Peter Christopher

First published in Great Britain by
Hodder & Stoughton Publishers,
Mill Road, Dunton Green, Sevenoaks, Kent TN13 2YA

British Library Cataloguing-in-Publication Data
Dyson, John
  Westward with Columbus.—(Time Quest)
  I. Title II. Series
  910.4

ISBN 0-340-55564-5

Design and Art Direction: Gordon Sibley Design Inc.
Illustration: Greg Ruhl, Ken Marschall, Wesley Lowe
Maps and Diagrams: Jack McMaster, Margo Stahl
Editorial Director: Hugh M. Brewster
Manuscript Editor: Shelley Tanaka
Project Editors: Nan Froman, Mireille Majoor
Production Director: Susan Barrable
Production Assistant: Donna Chong
Printer: Khai Wah Litho (Pte) Limited

Endpapers: Columbus sails with a fleet of seventeen ships on his second voyage to the New World.

Previous page: The crest of Christopher Columbus, given to him by the king and queen after his first successful voyage in 1492.

Right: Wind fills the sails of the new *Niña* as we set out across the Atlantic.

Overleaf: This woodcut shows a bustling seaport in Columbus's day.

Produced by Madison Press Books
40 Madison Avenue
Toronto, Ontario
Canada M5R 2S1   *Printed in Singapore*

WESTWARD WITH

COLUMBUS

Text by John Dyson

Photographs by Peter Christopher

A HODDER & STOUGHTON / MADISON PRESS BOOK

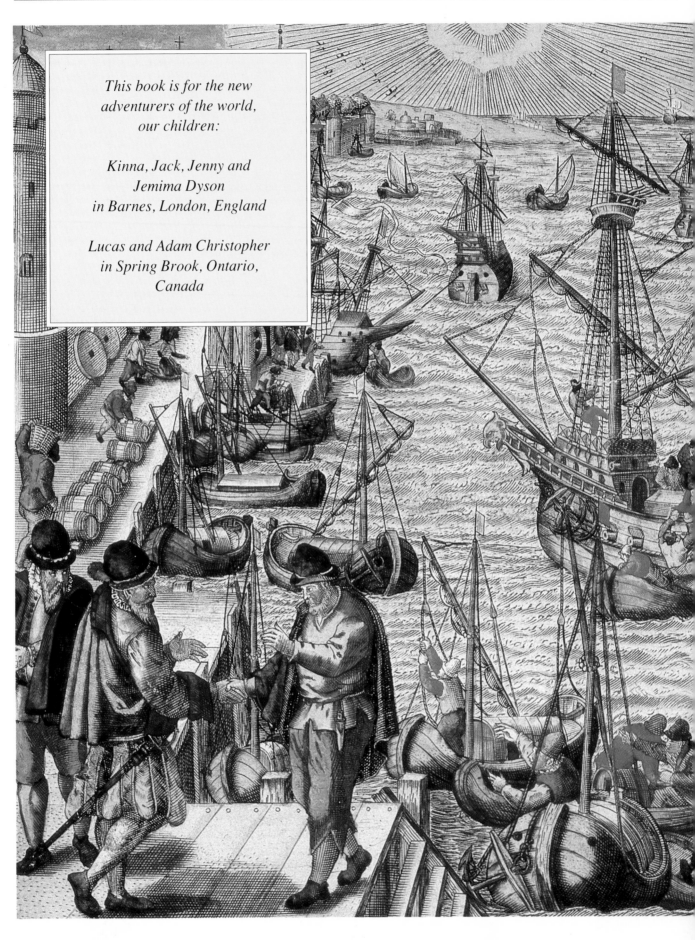

*This book is for the new
adventurers of the world,
our children:*

*Kinna, Jack, Jenny and
Jemima Dyson
in Barnes, London, England*

*Lucas and Adam Christopher
in Spring Brook, Ontario,
Canada*

CONTENTS

As the sun rises on August 3, 1492, Christopher Columbus and his fleet of wooden sailing ships, the *Santa María*, *Pinta* and *Niña*, leave Spain heading down the River Tinto toward the open sea. Columbus has dreamed of making this voyage for years. He is convinced that if he sails across the "sea of darkness" he will find a land full of gold. Soon power, riches and glory will be his.

Nearly five hundred years later, John Dyson, Dr. Coin and a crew of Spanish students retrace Columbus's voyage across the vast Atlantic aboard a replica of the *Niña*. Sailing as Columbus did with no engine or modern comforts, they finally reach the turquoise waters and emerald islands of the New World. With great excitement they row the ship's boat to shore, reliving that moment in history when people from two different branches of the human race came face to face.

CHAPTER ONE

CHRISTOPHER COLUMBUS SAILS AGAIN

Cadiz, Spain, November 9, 1988

Columbus's three ships leave Spain in 1492 *(top)*. The new *Niña* *(above)* as I first saw her in Cadiz.

Sitting among the sleek white yachts gleaming in the morning sunshine, the tubby wooden vessel in the Cadiz marina looked like a dirty old shoe. But she made my heart leap with excitement.

I was looking at a replica of the caravel *Niña*—one of the three ships that Christopher Columbus had taken on his first voyage of discovery to America.

I took in every feature—her blunt black bow, her three stumpy masts leaning at odd angles, her rough timbers coated with sticky black tar. She was not beautiful, but for me, seeing this ship was like a dream come true.

At school I had read how Columbus, the son of a poor wool weaver, had started his seaman's career as a humble ship's boy. And I had been told how, five hundred years ago, when many people thought that a ship could fall off the edge of the earth, Columbus had bravely turned his fleet away from the known land and discovered a whole new world on the other side of the ocean.

As a writer, I had voyaged to many corners of the world in everything from a polar icebreaker and a South Seas schooner to a naval submarine. But I had never sailed in a vessel like the *Niña*.

The tide was low, and there was no ladder down to the ship. I scrambled down a rope, grazing my knees on the stone wall of the wharf. The instant I stepped on board, my blood began to tingle.

I felt as if I had stepped into a different world—the world of Columbus the mariner. I put my hands on the sturdy wooden tiller and gazed out over the blue waters of the bay. How would it feel, I wondered, to steer across an empty ocean into the unknown in this tiny wooden sailing ship?

A sudden scraping sound beneath my feet startled me back to the present. Slowly, the heavy wooden cover of the hatchway leading to the hold was pushed back, and a man climbed out of the dark interior. It was Dr. Luís Coin, the person I had come to Spain to meet.

Dr. Coin was a long-time sea captain who had voyaged all over the world. Like me, he had the sea in his blood and had read everything there was to read about the voyages of Columbus. Most historians believed that, inspired by a hunch, Columbus had sailed due west from the Canary Islands until he found land that no European had been to before.

But Dr. Coin was puzzled by this version of Columbus's story. From his experience as a seaman he knew it was impossible for the famous explorer to have met the headwinds and contrary currents following the route that his diary describes. And how, for example, could Columbus have sighted shore birds like pelicans and ducks when, according to the diary, he was in the middle of the Atlantic Ocean?

The quest for the truth about Columbus became Dr. Coin's passion. For sixteen years he spent hours and hours digging for facts in dusty archives and poring over charts and old books of navigation. The result was an 800-page report that he presented to eight of Spain's most respected historians. His conclusions were so convincing that he was awarded a doctorate of history for his work.

Now I sat on the hot tarred deck of the *Niña*

Aboard the new *Niña*, Dr. Coin and I discuss our plan to voyage across the Atlantic as Columbus did.

and listened to Dr. Coin explain his remarkable findings. And for the first time I felt that I knew what had really happened on that historic voyage.

According to Dr. Coin, Columbus did not sail due west across the Atlantic until he found the New World. Instead, he took a route that dipped far to the south into enemy Portuguese waters. He then inserted false distances and directions into his diary to make it look as if he were sailing west of the Canary Islands. This way, if he were captured by the Portuguese, he could claim that storms or contrary winds had pushed him into their zone.

Dr. Coin's research also gave convincing new support to an idea that had been around since the time Christopher Columbus was alive. He believed that the world's most famous explorer followed a secret map—a map that he had obtained from someone who had actually been to the New World before him.

In the course of his research, Dr. Coin raised money to build a replica of the *Niña*—the smallest ship of the fleet, and the one Columbus liked best.

As I listened to Dr. Coin's story, with the tangy smells of tar and rope in my nostrils, a wild idea began to dawn in my mind.

"What if we tried to sail this new *Niña* across the Atlantic?" I said hesitantly. "We could take the southerly route—the route you think Columbus really took. And we would see for ourselves what a long sea voyage might have been like five hundred years ago."

Dr. Coin nodded slowly. "That is my dream," he said.

Then he carefully explained what it would mean to sail like Columbus.

"Sailing conditions in 1492 were quite primitive," he warned. "If our voyage is to be authentic,

BUILDING A CARAVEL

Caravels are small, fast sailing ships that were used by the Spanish and Portuguese in the fifteenth century. The picture *(right)* shows how ship builders set up the ribs before nailing on the planks of these ships. Our replica caravel, the *Niña*, was built in the same way.

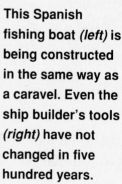

This Spanish fishing boat *(left)* is being constructed in the same way as a caravel. Even the ship builder's tools *(right)* have not changed in five hundred years.

we will have no engine to get us out of trouble in storms or to help us along on days when there is no wind. There will be no beds on board—not even a hammock, because they weren't discovered until Columbus reached the New World. And we will have to carry our fresh meat alive in cages. There were no refrigerators in Columbus's time. And no bathrooms."

As I heard Dr. Coin describe the risks, the cramped quarters and the many hardships, my heart beat faster.

Christopher Columbus's voyage had changed the course of history. No matter how tough it might be, the chance to sail in his wake was irresistible.

It took more than two years to repair the *Niña*, find a crew and get the little caravel ready for the voyage. But at last, soon after dawn on June 9, 1990, we heaved up our anchor. As her big square sails were hoisted and bellied in the wind, the *Niña* looked like an old painting that had magically come to life.

Standing on the deck of the caravel, the rail barely reaching my knees, I wondered what Columbus would have thought of the crowd that waved us off, most of them wearing T-shirts and jeans. What would he have said about the white high-rise buildings lining the Spanish shore, and the gigantic tankers anchored in the bay?

But soon these trappings of civilization were left behind. In five hundred years, little has changed at sea. The waves were just as blue and wet for us as they were for Columbus.

The rope pulleys squealed like gulls, and the *Niña* began to forge ahead, bound on a 4,000-mile (6,400-kilometre) adventure. That night we sailed not far from the little town of Pálos de la Frontera, the town from which Columbus and his fleet had set out so long ago. As I listened to the white wave bubbling around the bow, I wondered what songs it would sing to us about that historic voyage that had changed the face of the world.

Skilfully perched on the side of the ship, a crewmember loads supplies onto the new *Niña*.

CHAPTER TWO

"THE MADMAN OF GENOA IS BACK!"

Pálos de la Frontera, Spain, May 23, 1492

The sudden peal of the church bells startled Pedro as they rang out over the little town of Pálos de la Frontera.

The young boy put down the shrimping nets he was unloading and squinted up the hill in the direction of the church. What could be wrong? It wasn't time for Mass. Were the enemy Portuguese attacking from the other side of the frontier?

Already people had begun to head up the grassy bluff toward the church to see what was happening. Farmers and vine-growers left their fields and hurried into town. From the handful of ships anchored in the River Tinto, small boats pushed out and headed for shore with splashing oars.

"Pedro! Give us a hand!" The shout came from a boat belonging to the Niño family's caravel, which they called the *Niña*. It was Peralonso Niño, standing up and beckoning to the boy. Peralonso's older brother, Juan, rowed the boat with powerful strokes.

Pedro untangled himself from

CHRISTOPHER COLUMBUS

When Christopher Columbus was fourteen he left his childhood home in Genoa and went to sea as a ship's boy. By the time he was thirty-two he had sailed as far north as England, and as far south as Guinea, in Africa. Because the world is round, Columbus believed he could reach the eastern shores of Asia by sailing west. Such a voyage would win him wealth, power and glory. For years Columbus tried to gain support for his idea, and in 1492, Queen Isabella of Castile agreed to give him ships and money for his voyage.

his nets and waded across the expanse of soft low-tide mud. He pulled the boat in until it stuck, then sat on the ledge so Peralonso could climb on his back. Pedro carried his chuckling passenger to dry land before going back to help Juan, a beefy, cranky man.

"One speck of dirt on these stockings, boy, and I'll tie you to a post and whip you raw!" Juan threatened as he heaved his huge bulk onto the boy's back. Pedro sank to his knees in the soft mud and staggered to shore, gritting his teeth to keep his legs from buckling.

"What is it? What's going on?" he asked Peralonso as he set Juan down.

"Didn't you hear? That crazy foreigner is back in town. Columbus!"

Even Pedro knew about Christopher Columbus. The madman of Genoa had been to Pálos many times before. Pedro had seen the tall, white-haired stranger ambling around town,

Right: **Pedro pulls the boat carrying the Niño brothers to shore.**

his cloak threadbare, his boots falling apart. The man would come down to the river to talk to the other seamen. His eyes would burn feverishly as he spoke of the great wealth and fame that awaited the first navigator who dared to set his course westward. The foreigner actually believed that if he sailed west across the ocean, he would find land on the far side—a land full of gold and other fabulous riches.

But Columbus had not been in town for some time. Some said he was at court, trying to interest the king and queen in his wild idea. The man was clearly a lunatic.

"But what is he doing here this time?" Pedro asked breathlessly. He was trying to keep up with the long strides of the Niño brothers as they joined the procession up to the church.

"They say the Genoese has finally won royal approval for his mad scheme to cross the ocean," Peralonso muttered. "But I'm sure the king and queen would never support such a crazy idea. No ship in the world can sail that far."

The church was crowded. It seemed that every citizen of Pálos was present. Pedro left a trail of muddy footprints on the cool floor as he slipped into a pew beside the Niño brothers.

The crowd hushed as the tall figure of Columbus walked to the front of the church. Pedro craned his neck to get a better look.

But the sight of the man made him blink in astonishment. This didn't look like the shabby stranger that he and the other boys had followed in the streets—the ridiculous figure they had made fun of and thrown stones at. Columbus now stood tall and dignified. He was accompanied by a group of officials and Father Juan Pérez, the most respected monk in the town.

Townspeople flock into the church at Pálos *(below)* to hear a local official read the royal edict telling them to supply Columbus with ships and provisions *(left)*. The photo *(above)* shows the doorway of the church in Pálos today.

Chains of thick gold adorned Columbus's neck, and he wore fine new shoes on his feet.

Silence fell as the town's attorney began to read the royal edict. Indeed, the people of Pálos were commanded by the king and queen to make ready two caravels within ten days. The ships were to be fully manned and provided with food for a year. Then they were to be put at Columbus's disposal for a voyage "to certain parts of the Ocean Sea."

Pedro looked up at Peralonso Niño. The man's eyes were narrowed in concentration as he thoughtfully stroked his black beard. Then the boy looked back at Columbus. The hint of a smile played at the edges of the mariner's mouth. The gaze in his gray eyes was steely and clear.

What would it be like to sail under a man like this, Pedro wondered. Were there really treasures to be found on the other side of the ocean?

Becoming a seaman was Pedro's dream. He had already spent so much time around boats that caravels and cargo ships were as familiar to him as his own home. He could tie any knot at lightning speed and weave a fishing net and shinny to the top of a mast as easily as walking.

Pedro couldn't wait until he was old enough to go to sea himself. Peralonso Niño had promised him that in another year or two, he might be able to serve as ship's boy on the *Niña*.

For the next several days Pedro went about his business of doing odd jobs for sailors in the port, but he kept his ears and eyes open. He heard the men grumbling and complaining about the royal orders and Columbus's plans.

"Who will sign on for a voyage to suicide? Not me!" one old sailor said, shaking his head.

"I'm no coward," said another. "I've stared

into many a knife blade of the cursed Portuguese, but they'll burn me at the stake before I sail with the madman of Genoa!"

The ten-day deadline passed almost unnoticed. Columbus was seen talking to seamen in the town,

KING FERDINAND AND QUEEN ISABELLA

When Isabella married Ferdinand two of the most powerful kingdoms in Spain, Castile and Aragon, were united. The Christian king and queen had a common purpose—to drive the Muslims and Jews out of their land. For years the queen's attention was devoted to this cause. But in 1492 she agreed to back Columbus's dream of sailing across the ocean.

his face pale with anger. The only man willing to go on the voyage was Bartolomeo Torres. A few weeks earlier, Torres had stabbed the town crier of Pálos to death. To avoid being executed he had volunteered to sail with the fleet, for the queen had told Columbus to pardon any criminal who joined his crew. But the other men of Pálos, as stubborn as they were tough, seemed to be unmoved by Columbus's pleading.

edro was sitting on the shore mending ropes for the *Niña* when he spotted a familiar sail gliding up the river. It was the ship of Martín Alonso Pinzón, returning from Sicily with a cargo of grain. A grizzled sailor who had had more than his share of sea fights and long voyages, Martín Alonso was one of the town's most respected captains. He and his three brothers owned several ships, and many of the sailors in port worked for him.

A short, powerful man with broad shoulders, Martín Alonso had just stepped ashore when he was summoned to call on Father Pérez. Before long he returned, his back rigid with anger and determination. Standing up on the edge of a brick water trough, his hands on his hips, he addressed the men.

"You men of Pálos disappoint me!" he raged. "The king and queen —whom God protect!— selected us for a noble undertaking, and you have refused! I am ashamed of you!"

Pedro watched the men shuffle their feet and look at the ground.

"Do you want to know who will sail with the man from Genoa?" The captain beat his fist on his broad chest. "Me! I am proud to sail in his fleet,

Sea captain Martín Alonso Pinzón encouraged the men of Pálos to sail with Christopher Columbus.

and so are my brothers. Sailors of Pálos, we are being offered a chance for fame and glory. Come with us, and we'll all be rich!"

That night, Pedro walked home thinking of Martín Alonso's words. He and his mother lived in the corner of a stable that belonged to the Niño family. His mother looked

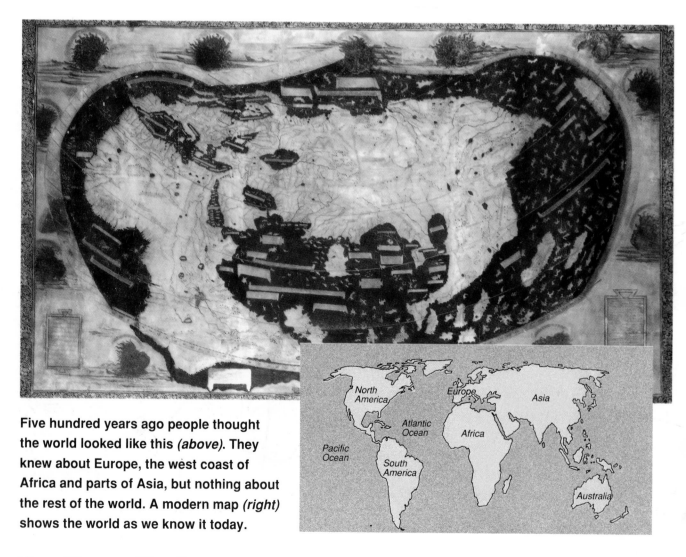

Five hundred years ago people thought the world looked like this *(above)*. They knew about Europe, the west coast of Africa and parts of Asia, but nothing about the rest of the world. A modern map *(right)* shows the world as we know it today.

after their goats and grew vegetables.

Suddenly a voice came out of the night behind him. It was Peralonso Niño.

"How old are you, boy?" the man asked.

"Twelve. Thirteen, maybe." Pedro straightened his shoulders and lifted his chin. "Old enough to go to sea."

"Well, you may have your chance sooner than you think." Even in the soft darkness the boy could see the glint in Peralonso's eyes.

"What do you mean?"

"I've just signed on as navigator of Columbus's ship. And you, boy, can sail as *grommet* with me and the admiral. I can tell you now it'll be backbreaking work. A boy is no better than a slave on a ship. But if you think you're ready..."

Pedro's jaw dropped with disbelief. It was the moment he had been dreaming of for years. To be an apprentice seaman, to go on a real voyage with Peralonso...

He nodded. Peralonso laughed and clapped his big hand on the boy's shoulder.

"Good, then," he said. "I'll see you in the morning." His heavy steps echoed down the cobblestoned street as he strode toward the tavern.

Pedro stood stock still for a moment, his thoughts whirling. Then he turned and carried on home, not knowing whether the fierce beating of his heart was from joy or fear.

What, he wondered, would his mother say when she heard he was going to sail into the unknown with the madman of Genoa?

The next few weeks were filled with activity as the three ships of the fleet were made ready. The *Niña* and the *Pinta* were small caravels that could not carry enough food and water for a long voyage. So for his third ship Columbus had to charter a bigger and clumsier cargo vessel that he named *Santa María*.

When Pedro climbed on board the *Santa María* for the first time, he couldn't believe his luck. She was twice the size of the caravels, with three masts and square sails. This would be the flagship—the ship that Columbus himself would captain, while he would also be in charge of the whole fleet. Juan de la Cosa, the ship's owner, would be second-in-command over the ship's crew of forty, and Peralonso Niño would be the navigator.

The sailors ran the ships ashore at high tide. When the tide left them high and dry on the mud, they were hauled on their sides, first one way, then the other, and the planks were scraped of weed and painted with tar to make them watertight.

Carlos, a young crewmember on the new *Niña*, winds twine around the end of a rope to keep it from unraveling.

Meanwhile, Pedro and the other boys in the crew had the messy job of scrubbing out the stinking bilges inside the ships with vinegar. Pedro learned to carry a rock in his pocket to squash the thousands of cockroaches he found.

Then the sailors loaded provisions for a year's voyaging. There were sacks of *vizcocho*, a bread made with salt water so it would keep, then baked into cakes as hard and flat as roof tiles. There were barrels of strong wine which had a golden hue, jars of olive oil and vinegar, long strings of garlic and onions, casks of salted sardines and bags of dried beans and rice.

All over Pálos the townspeople strung fish out on lines to dry in the withering sunshine. They butchered cows and pigs and salted the meat down in barrels.

Top: Columbus receives a last blessing before sailing into the unknown. *Above:* Like Columbus, we carried live animals on board.

For the admiral and his officials there were a few luxuries such as smoke-cured hams, sheep and goat cheeses, bags of raisins, stone jars of honey and quince jelly. There were cooking pots, candles, swords, guns and spare planks.

Finally, bundles of wood for the cooking fires were crammed into every available space, and the big water casks were filled from the old Roman fountain on the foreshore before being rolled down the beach and towed out to the waiting ships.

At last the fleet was ready to sail. The shore was filled with people, waving and whistling. As Pedro got ready to climb into the *Santa María*'s boat to row the crew out to the ship, he saw his mother push her way through the crowd. Pedro stood tall. He hoped she wouldn't break down and weep in front of everyone.

But his mother simply looked into his face, smiled sadly, and pressed a small round object into his hand.

It was a tiny bell—the kind tied to the legs of hunting hawks.

Pedro looked up, not knowing what to say. But his mother had already disappeared into the large crowd.

Quickly he got into the boat. Columbus climbed aboard, his royal officials crowding in behind him. Pedro stared at the admiral's ruddy complexion, high cheekbones and clear eyes. It did not look like the face of a madman.

Throughout the afternoon, the *Santa María* led the two caravels down the River Tinto toward the sea. Pedro watched as the red-roofed monastery high on the bank disappeared. From within its walls came the chime of a bell.

In the morning, the real voyage would begin. The three vessels would turn away from the land and set their course toward the open sea.

The *Santa María*, *Pinta* and *Niña* turn their bows away from Spain on the first day of their voyage.

"ALL HANDS ON DECK!"

River Tinto, Spain, August 3, 1492

P edro woke when the thick rope he was using as a pillow was suddenly yanked out from under him and dragged away along the deck. It was still dark, but in the east the sky was growing pale with the promise of dawn.

On the *Santa María*, the seamen were beginning to bustle about their tasks. The flagship's bell rang loudly, and Juan de la Cosa, the second-in-command, shouted across the water to the two caravels, *Pinta* and *Niña*. "Make sail! Make sail!"

Pedro helped to loosen the ropes binding the

As dawn breaks *(top)*, a sailor raises sails on the *Niña (above)*.

sails. As the smallest and youngest, he was sent to the end of the yardarm hanging over the black water. Clinging on like a monkey, he undid the ropes with his teeth and one hand.

On the poop deck, the high deck at the stern of the ship, Columbus judged the tide streaming around them and the wind fanning across the water from the far bank. Then he nodded to Juan de la Cosa, who bellowed through his cupped hands, "Man the capstan!"

While seamen pushed on long wooden handles to pull in the heavy anchor rope, Pedro slithered through an opening in the deck into the rope locker. It was pitch-black and stank of rotten fish. As the muddy anchor rope slowly came in, Pedro laid it flat so that it did not build up into a tangled heap.

At last he heard the bump of the anchor hitting the bow. He climbed out of the rope locker, blinking in the daylight. The deck was slimy with mud and seaweed from the anchor rope.

"You, boy!" It was Peralonso Niño, and he was not in his usual friendly mood. "Wash down the deck and be quick about it!"

Pedro dipped a bucket over the side, but when he tossed the water along the planks, it splashed a rough, black-bearded man who was coiling a rope. The seaman jumped at Pedro and gave him a stinging smack on the ear.

"Do that again and you're fish bait!" the man hissed.

Pedro stumbled backward in his hurry to get away. He knew the man. It was Bartolomeo Torres, the murderer.

Bartolomeo was one crewmember, Pedro decided, he would try to avoid.

The sun climbed into the sky like a hot gold ducat. The sails began to swell, and the oars were brought in as the fleet left the mouth of the river.

All morning Pedro fetched water for the men, scrubbed the deck, fed the hens and hauled wood to keep the cook's fire going. He was so busy that he hardly noticed the hills of Spain dropping astern. High above his head, the sails bellied into hard curves. Every rope trembled with strain. A white wave bubbled around the ship's bow, and curls of foam spun along the tarred planks. The deck tilted as the *Santa María* leaned under the press of wind. Then she moved up and down as the bow cut into the Atlantic swells.

Pedro's stomach lurched as the sinewy motion of the ship sent him staggering from one side of the deck to the other. A wave of nausea swept over him so fast that when his legs buckled he barely had time to grab the rail before throwing up over the side.

When he had finished being sick, he opened

his eyes and found himself staring at the knees of Peralonso Niño.

"Get used to it, boy," the older man said, not unkindly. "This sea is like a mother's arms compared with what we'll see farther out."

In the afternoon, the *Santa María*'s crew was divided into three watches, or "guards," which would take turns running the ship. Every four

We washed down the deck several times a day to keep the wooden planks from splitting in the sun.

hours, day and night, the watches changed. For most of the men, this meant that after four hours on watch they had eight hours to eat, sleep and wash their clothes. But for the ship's boys, the work was never done.

Columbus had only a sandglass to keep track of time *(left)* but we had digital watches. To signal changes of duty-watch we rang the bell *(right).*

One of Pedro's jobs on watch was to guard the sandglass—the ship's only clock. Every half hour, when it emptied, he turned the glass upside down and rang the bell. Eight bells signaled the end of four hours, when the watch changed.

"A word of warning," Peralonso told Pedro sternly. "If you fall asleep and miss the time, every man on board will be after you with a rope's end—including me!"

That night, lying on his thin mat in the hold beneath the deck, Pedro felt as if he were trying to sleep on a horse galloping through a dark cave. The deck swooped upward, pressing him into the planks. Then it suddenly dropped, leaving him in mid-air. As his body fell, it collided with the deck coming up again. He was soon a mass of raw spots and bruises.

The noise in the hold was terrific. The sea roared along the planks beside his head. Water slapped and gurgled in the bilges beneath his mat, and the timbers creaked and groaned.

He didn't know how long he had been asleep when he was awakened by a shout. "All hands! All hands on deck!"

The men clawed their way over Pedro on their way to the ladder, elbows and knees digging into him. But when he tried to get up, he found his head glued to the spot. The more he tried to move, the more it hurt.

Pedro felt the back of his head. His hair was glued to the sticky black tar that coated the whole ship inside and out.

Quickly he pulled his knife from the sheath on his belt and sawed the blade through his hair. Then he scrambled up the ladder behind the others.

But he was not prepared for the world that greeted him.

A fierce squall was blasting the ship with wind and rain. The *Santa María* lay so far over that Pedro's feet skidded out from under him. Black waves capped with feathers of white rose steeply on either side.

Bumping together in the wild, wet darkness, the men ran to the ropes. Swollen with water, the coils were heavy and stiff. It seemed to take hours before the huge mainsail was inched to the deck and lashed down.

The ship rode more easily now, and at least there was less danger of capsizing. His wet clothes rattling on his shivering body and his eyes red from the blasts of wind and salt water, Pedro began to follow the other sailors back down to the hold. Even his little tar-smeared mat seemed inviting now.

He had barely got one foot through the hatch when eight bells sounded. It was four o'clock in the morning. Time for his watch.

"You, boy!" a gruff voice said. "Up to the top with you!"

Blinking back tears of exhaustion, Pedro gripped the slippery rope and wriggled up to the platform near the top of the mast, high above the deck. Fifty feet (fifteen metres) up, every sway and dip of the ship seemed to bring his stomach up into his throat. Though he had shinnied up many a

Right: **Pedro clings to wet ropes at the top of the mast to keep from toppling overboard as he gazes at the pitching deck beneath him.**

mainmast in the port at Pálos, he had never done so on a fiercely rolling ship at night.

Sitting on the edge of the swinging platform, Pedro wrapped his arms and feet around as many different ropes as he could and miserably tried to keep his eyes open for the sight of a Portuguese warship or pirate ship bent on plunder. He knew that if he didn't stay awake, he could easily lose his seat and plunge into the black sea hissing far below.

In the days that followed, Pedro grew accustomed to the hard routine of the seafarer. He got used to shuffling along the deck with his feet placed wide apart. He learned the sailor's knack of falling asleep the instant his head touched the deck, no matter what was going on around him. He finally stopped being seasick.

The tiny hawk's bell that his mother had given him hung around his neck on a piece of string. Soon it was only when it bumped against his chest, tinkling, that he was reminded of the world he had left behind.

Already he felt as though the ship was his home, the other crewmembers his family, and Columbus their inspired leader.

Standing on the poop deck with his white hair streaming in the wind, the admiral's gaze moved constantly between the flagship's sails and the two caravels sailing a few hundred yards on either side. He looked confident and noble—like a man on a mission for God. Soon, Pedro felt sure, their voyage would bring glory and riches to them all.

But on the fifth day, as the fleet headed southwest toward the island of Gomera in the Canary Islands—their final stop before heading into the open ocean—there was trouble.

The *Pinta*'s rudder broke. On the *Santa María*, Peralonso Niño heard the news and glanced anxiously toward the east. The bleak, empty coast of Africa was just in sight. Without a rudder, the wind could easily push the stricken caravel into the rocks where she would be smashed to pieces.

(continued on page 30)

A Day Aboard The New *Niña*

The cook woke us up at 7:30 a.m. and we quickly wriggled into damp clothes. Those on watch at 8 a.m. ate breakfast first and then began navigation, steering and lookout duties. Off watch we played dominoes or cards. At sunset we ate supper and then sang songs before turning in for a short sleep until our next watch.

Carlos keeps an eye on the compass *(above left)* **while Fernanda and Mata hoist the heavy mainsail** *(above right).*

Above: We ate our main meal of rice or bean soup, olives and cheese at midday. Sometimes we caught and fried fish *(right)* and on a few occasions we cooked the chickens we had brought on board *(bottom right).*

Left: Buckets of salty water were all that we had to cool ourselves off or bathe in.

THE ADMIRAL'S FLEET

hristopher Columbus sailed to the New World in 1492 with a fleet of three ships—the *Santa María*, *Pinta* and *Niña*. The *Santa María* is known as the flagship because she carried the admiral, Columbus himself. But the *Niña* was the ship Columbus liked best because she brought the men home to Spain safely through violent storms. The new *Niña (bottom right)* is an exact replica of Columbus's caravel. We slept on bare boards in the hold, beneath the deck, which we reached by going through the hatchways. The caravel was just sixty-four feet long.

THE SANTA MARÍA

Top: We flew Queen Isabella's flag from the mast of the *Niña*.
Above: Our modern compass was ten times more accurate than the one carried by Columbus.

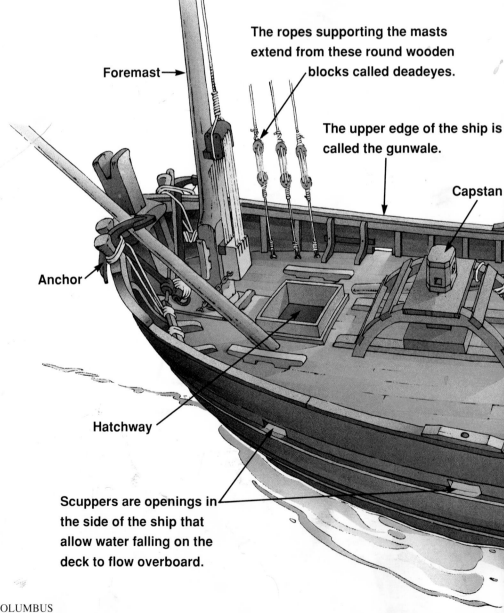

Foremast →

The ropes supporting the masts extend from these round wooden blocks called deadeyes.

The upper edge of the ship is called the gunwale.

Capstan

Anchor

Hatchway

Scuppers are openings in the side of the ship that allow water falling on the deck to flow overboard.

The *Santa María* was a slow, clumsy cargo ship. The *Pinta* and *Niña* were smaller vessels called caravels. Columbus switched the *Niña*'s tall triangular sails to broad square ones like those of the *Pinta* in the Canaries to take full advantage of the winds blowing across the Atlantic.

THE *PINTA*

THE *NIÑA*

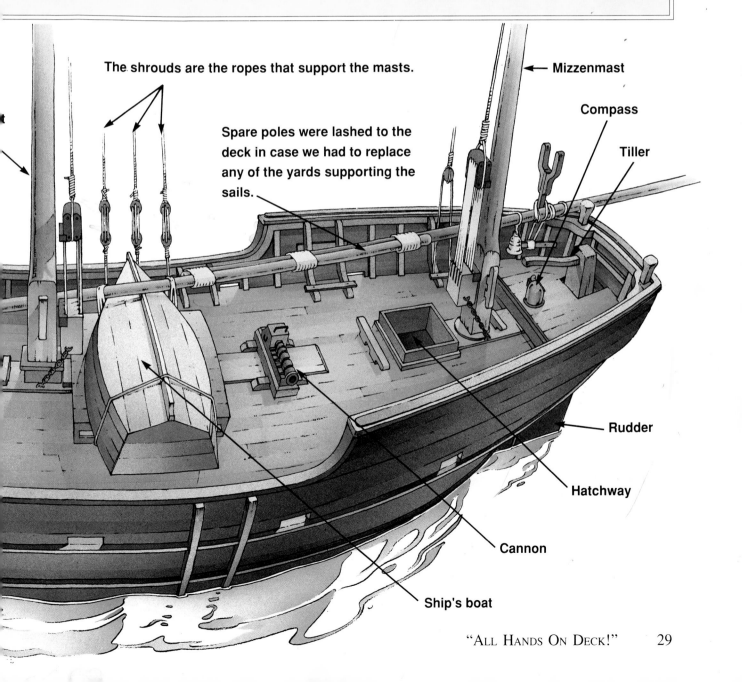

The shrouds are the ropes that support the masts.

Spare poles were lashed to the deck in case we had to replace any of the yards supporting the sails.

← Mizzenmast

Compass

Tiller

Rudder

Hatchway

Cannon

Ship's boat

(continued from page 26)

Repairs were made in time for the ships to claw their way clear of the killer coast, but the following day the *Pinta*'s rudder fell off completely. The caravel could not be steered, and now the ship was leaking.

"Give me a ship built in Pálos and I'll show you a heap of firewood!" raged Columbus. Pedro had never seen the admiral in such a foul mood.

Then, just as the dark outline of the Canary Islands was sighted far to the west, the wind died.

For three days the ships rolled upon their own reflections. With every roll, their sails clapped like thunder. Every man was irritable and bad-tempered, especially Columbus.

When at last the wind returned, the admiral gave startling orders.

Two crewmembers make a spare tiller for the *Niña*. As in Columbus's day, we had to repair everything on the ship ourselves.

"We're hoisting sail," he shouted across the water to the crippled *Pinta*. "We shall push on to Gomera with the *Niña*. Catch up when you can!"

Instantly, Pedro saw the squat figure of Martín Alonso Pinzón spring onto the rail of the *Pinta*. His anger seemed to flame across the water.

"You cannot abandon my men to the mercy of the sea!" he shouted.

But Columbus turned a deaf ear to the Spanish captain. Flinging out an arm and pointing to the west, he merely replied, "Gomera!" Then he turned and shut himself up in his cabin.

A buzz of anger swept through the sailors of the *Santa María*. Even Pedro knew that by age-old custom a ship was duty bound to stick by another in trouble. The *Santa María* could have towed the *Pinta* to a safe port, or at least stayed close in case of need. Without a rudder, the small caravel was helpless.

What could the admiral be thinking of?

"He only cares about finding gold," Bartolomeo spat as he tested the blade of his dagger with his thumb. "What kind of a captain puts himself before his men?"

At dawn the high peak of Gomera was in sight. The island's little town of San Sebastian was the most westerly port in the known world. Here the fleet planned to take on its final supplies of food and water.

The *Santa María* and the *Niña* dropped anchor. Days passed, but the *Pinta* did not appear. For Pedro and the other boys who were sent ashore to gather firewood, the waiting seemed endless.

Had the admiral forgotten the purpose of their voyage? What was he waiting for? And why had he abandoned the *Pinta*, only to waste time in Gomera?

Finally, after two weeks, Columbus gave orders to sail to Grand Canary Island.

When they arrived they learned that, by a stroke of fate, the *Pinta* had reached the island only the day before. The caravel had spent sixteen days struggling to reach the shore, and her men said they were lucky to be alive.

Columbus finally decided to build a new rudder for the *Pinta*, and her leaking seams were repaired. Then all three ships sailed back to

Gomera to take on final supplies of firewood, fresh fish, cheese, vegetables and drinking water.

Fetching the water was Pedro's job, and he knew how important it was. Nobody knew how long it might be before they could obtain fresh water again. And without drinking water, the whole crew would quickly perish.

First he rowed the *Santa María*'s best boat to shore, where it was scrubbed out with fresh water. Then the boy had to scrub his bare feet and legs until they were pink and raw. Buckets of

Before leaving the Canaries *(bottom)* we filled the ship's boat with fresh water then transferred it by bucket into barrels in the hold *(below)*.

fresh well water were tipped into the boat, and when it was full, Pedro gingerly climbed in and sat down in the water. Paddling the tippy boat carefully, he made it safely back to the flagship, where the water was transferred, bucket by bucket, into the barrels down in the hold.

At last, on the morning of Thursday, September 6, 1492, Pedro said his last prayers with the other men in the little church by the shore. Then Christopher Columbus gave the orders that turned the bows of his little fleet toward the unknown horizon.

CHAPTER FOUR

ACROSS THE SEA OF DARKNESS

Columbus sails the ocean blue

Pedro's eyes followed the ship's wake that pointed a crooked finger toward the land they had left. The cliffs of Gomera were just a faint blue line. For the first time, he felt a hollowness in his stomach. All around him, men seemed to be sneaking glances at the island slipping astern.

How long would it be before they saw land again? What really lay beyond the western horizon? Could the old tales be true, that ships venturing into the

(Above) Ships being blown across the ocean by the winds. (Below) Columbus feared attacks by the Portuguese. Fierce sea battles were common in his day.

unknown would be eaten by sea monsters?

Pedro felt a warm, heavy hand on his shoulder. It was Peralonso Niño.

"I know what you're feeling, boy. I've voyaged as far as any man—north to England, south to the coast of Guinea. But even when we couldn't see it, we always knew the land was there, just out of sight. We always knew we could get wood and fresh water if we had to. This time, things are different."

"But...we'll find it, won't we? The land full of gold? The admiral's paradise?"

It was several moments before the older man spoke. "Nobody knows what lies under the sunset. No ship has ever turned away from the land to steer straight out into the green sea of darkness. Nobody knows how far we will have to go until we reach land again."

The admiral gave his orders to the helmsman. "We're changing course! Steer southwest!"

"Southwest? Into Portuguese waters?" Peralonso frowned. "If we're captured, the admiral will be taken to Portugal and hanged. And you and I, my boy, will be thrown overboard or put to the sword." He turned abruptly to head up to the poop deck. "Maybe the man truly is mad..." Pedro heard him mutter grimly under his breath.

"Boy, get aloft with you!" Juan de la Cosa ordered. "We need all the eyes we can get. We're heading into dangerous waters."

The three ships were sailing south when Pedro spotted a strange ship on the horizon. "Sail ho!" he cried.

It was another Spanish caravel. The *Santa María* spilled wind from her sails to slow down as the caravel turned alongside. Her captain pointed toward the southwest and shouted across the water. "Three Portuguese caravels just over the horizon! Armed and filled with men...! You're heading straight for them...!"

Pedro shuddered. It was just as Peralonso had feared. To make matters worse, the wind dropped. The *Santa María*, *Pinta* and *Niña* rocked helplessly on a glassy sea under the blistering sun,

Crewmembers on the *Niña* lower and roll up one of the sails.

while enemy ships lay just out of sight.

"Launch the boats," Columbus ordered. "We must put some distance between ourselves and the enemy."

All through the hot afternoon, all night and all the next day, they toiled at the oars, trying to tow the fleet northward back into Spanish waters. Soon Pedro's hands were blistered and raw, his face a fiery red. He had never worked so hard.

At last a line of ruffled blue was seen advancing across the shining sea. "Here comes the wind, praise God!" Peralonso shouted. The seamen hurriedly hoisted the boats aboard. The sails flapped, then filled, and the ships finally began to forge ahead.

Carlos, on lookout duty, enjoys the warm, steady trade winds that blew us westward for days.

Since the Portuguese fleet was blocking the way to the southwest, Columbus decided to try to slip by them unseen. He gave orders to sail west for a day before turning south again into Portuguese waters.

Pedro's neck prickled with fear when he heard the news. Their heavily laden ships would never outrun the Portuguese. Why were they going to risk all by heading into enemy waters, when the lands they were seeking lay to the west?

All day Pedro's aching eyes searched the horizon for the sight of enemy sails. But the only ships he saw were the *Pinta* and the *Niña*, always sailing ahead of the flagship because they were faster. In the *Santa María*, Juan de la Cosa kept the men busy in the hold, moving barrels of food and water so the ship would sail better.

On the eighth day at sea, as Pedro was about to shinny up the mast for his watch, he noticed two birds circling the ship. One was a little tern. The other was bigger—white with tail feathers forming two long spikes.

"It's a tropic bird," Columbus explained. "They're never seen far from land. That means

we're near the Cape Verde Islands. The Portuguese have a naval base there, so keep a good lookout, boy."

At last, nine days out, the fleet turned westward again. As the danger of capture disappeared behind them, the mood on the ship lightened. The men sang as they went about their work.

Even the admiral was in a good mood. He often had a kind word for Pedro when the boy took him his wine in the small cabin under the poop deck. There Pedro would find Columbus stooped over a desk fixed to the wall, smiling and busily writing in his daily journal. His long legs would be braced at a funny angle to stop his chair from sliding across the deck as the ship rolled.

Pedro never tired of watching the enormous waves rolling up from behind. One moment a steep wall of water capped with a line of breaking surf would seem ready to topple on board like a cartload of bricks. Then the stern of the ship soared toward the sky, the deck tilted steeply, and

Pedro would unthinkingly grab the nearest handhold...before the ship surged forward again, a wall of foam rising high on either side of her bow.

When the deck tilted at night, everyone slithered down the slope like seals on a beach. Then there would be loud grunts and curses. Pedro quickly learned not to choose a sleeping spot next to the hot-tempered Bartolomeo.

No birds were seen now. Occasionally Pedro spotted a jellyfish with its purple sail glinting in the sun, and once a slumbering sea turtle gave him a startled look as it bumped the side of the ship like a large green rock.

One evening, when he was tending the candle that lit the steering compass, an object thudded hard into his chest. There was a wet trail down the front of his shirt, and something was jumping on the deck between his feet.

He had been hit by a flying fish! Then more fish landed on deck. Pedro grabbed as many of the slippery creatures as he could and dropped them into a bucket. Marinated in vinegar, then fried, they would make a tasty change from the endless meals of beans.

As the days passed, Pedro began to find the routine of ship life numbing. Before long, it seemed as if only two things were ever on his mind. How long to the next meal? And when could he sleep?

The admiral's staff—officials who were on board to keep records and look after the interests of the king and queen—seemed to become especially ill-tempered, mainly because they had no work to do. They spent their days lolling on the deck—when they weren't being seasick, picking tar off their shoes or complaining about the food. When Pedro threw buckets of water over the deck to prevent the planks from cracking in the sun's

In his diary Columbus describes the flying fish he saw. Twenty-seven flying fish landed on our deck!

heat, these "gentlemen" threatened to slit his throat if he got so much as a drop of water on their fine clothes and shoes.

In the hold, cockroaches as long as Pedro's thumb scuttled over his body as he slept. There were rats, too. And when he broke open a chunk of hard bread, he saw little white worms crawling in it. But he was so hungry that he just closed his eyes and swallowed as quickly as he could.

On September 24, nineteen days after leaving Gomera, the fleet was barreling along in a strong breeze. Tired and hungry as usual, Pedro was almost in a trance as he fetched water for the cook. He barely noticed Bartolomeo squatting in the dank hold, surrounded by a circle of men.

"I don't care what the Genoese says. I won't sail another league," Bartolomeo declared, jabbing his knife savagely into a plank.

The men nodded. "We've sailed our 750 leagues, just as we agreed. We must turn back."

"No easy task it'll be, too, against this wind!"

How Columbus Found His Way

To navigate Columbus steered his ships by compass, estimated how many miles they sailed each day, and plotted his position on a chart. He also carried a quadrant, an instrument which measured the angle of the Pole star *(below right)*. The sextant we carried five centuries later *(below left)* developed from the quadrant. We used it to "shoot" the sun and stars and calculate our exact position on the chart.

Pedro's ears pricked up. Turn back? But they had come so far. How could they return to Spain with nothing to show for their efforts?

"What about the admiral?" one man asked.

"The admiral was never more than a lunatic with a crazy idea. This is a fool's voyage."

"Besides, there are more than thirty of us against him. We can heave him over the side if he doesn't turn the fleet around."

"We'll tell the queen he fell overboard while observing the stars," laughed Bartolomeo.

All the next day the men's anger simmered. Just before sunset, the two caravels approached the *Santa María* as usual for orders.

"My men want to turn back," Columbus shouted across the water to Martín Alonso, the captain of the *Pinta*. "I say we carry on."

"We've completed our contract!" yelled Juan de la Cosa.

"The pilots are wrong," Columbus argued. "We haven't covered 750 leagues, and that is where we'll find the land we seek."

"How can you be so sure?" Martín Alonso shouted back.

The lines around the admiral's mouth tightened. Columbus hesitated before he spoke. "I have a map!"

Even from where he stood, Pedro could see Martín Alonso's eyebrows go up. Finally the stocky captain called sternly, "Show me this map."

Columbus said nothing for a moment. Then he turned without a word and went to his cabin.

When he returned, he held a rolled-up object wrapped in oil-cloth. A line was thrown to the *Pinta*, and the map was strung on the line and sent across to the caravel. Martín Alonso disappeared into his own cabin to study it, then reappeared and faced the men who were ranged along the flagship's side.

"The king and queen have entrusted us with a great and important mission," he said. "This is a discovery voyage, not a trading trip. We will sail on for as long as we have food and water, and as long as we are in good health."

The men on the *Santa María* muttered angrily among themselves. Then Martín Alonso put his hands squarely on his hips, his swarthy face growing dark with anger.

"And if there's any trouble," he roared, "I'll be over there with my brothers to hang a few of you from the mast!"

At this the men went sulkily back to work, preparing the ship for the night. The wind was now a faint breeze. The sun was sinking quickly, a brilliant fireball.

Suddenly Pedro heard a great shout. It was Martín Alonso, pointing toward the southwest.

"Land ahead!" he cried. "I see land!"

Right: **Pedro overhears Bartolomeo and the others plotting against the admiral.**

COLUMBUS HAS THREE DAYS TO LIVE

"Let's feed him to the sharks!"

edro screwed up his eyes against the glare of the setting sun. Sure enough, a hazy shape could be seen on the southwest horizon. Too low and solid to be a cloud, too big to be a ship...

It *had* to be land!

Christopher Columbus took one long look at the distant land. Then he fell to his knees and gave thanks to God.

Our first sight of land *(top)*. When the crew of the *Santa María* saw land they fell to their knees *(above)*.

All around him, men were clapping one another on the back and laughing. In the *Niña*, some climbed the rigging for a better look. In the *Pinta*, Martín Alonso Pinzón led his men in singing a hymn.

As the sun sank into the sea, the distant land stood out more sharply against the brilliant sky. It appeared to be an island several miles long. Then the glow of the tropical sunset faded like a dying fire, and the captains gave orders for sails to be lowered. It was dangerous to sail toward unknown land in darkness. They would have to wait until daylight.

As twilight swept over the sky and the three little ships stopped dead in the water, Pedro stripped off his clothes and leapt joyfully over the side for a swim. A school of dolphins came for a look. "They're a good omen," said Peralonso.

Few men slept that night. The admiral never left the deck. He prowled restlessly up and down, a smile lighting his normally grave expression. There was no talk of throwing him overboard now.

Before dawn, Pedro climbed to his lookout station up the mast. The top was already crowded with men. But when they gazed into the brightening shadows in the west, the horizon was empty.

The new-found land had disappeared.

The men's faces fell in disbelief and disappointment. Pedro could have wept. But the admiral simply said, "We have found land where I expected. Hoist the mainsail. Steer west!"

Pedro looked at Columbus in surprise. The land had been seen to the southwest. If they sailed west, wouldn't they miss it?

"There's more land to the west. We'll soon find it," Columbus promised.

But day followed day, and the wide sea remained empty.

When the winds began to come from directly ahead, the ships zigzagged back and forth, making little progress. But the men didn't mind. Through the many days of voyaging with the wind at their backs they had worried how they would fight against it when sailing home. A wind from the

west was a hopeful sign that they would get back to Spain more easily.

The sea was often flat and glassy, the sky hazy or gray. When a heavy rain swept over the ships, Pedro stood out in it so the blast of chilly fresh water would wash the sticky salt off his skin.

The air was so damp that mold appeared like green fur on the bread. The thick stench from the bilge water sloshing around under the hold filled Pedro's throat until he practically choked.

When Columbus saw land his men dived over the side for a swim. We too swam in calm waters.

Tempers flared. After an argument about a piece of moldy bread, Bartolomeo slashed the boatswain's arm with his dagger. The powerful boatswain turned like a shark and attacked the Pálos murderer with a length of wood. He would have beaten his brains out if the master-at-arms had not drawn his sword and separated the men.

Glaring and snarling like wolves on chains, the two men spent four days manacled to the deck while the boys were ordered to feed them nothing but water.

A week passed. Once again, just before dark, Martín Alonso reported that he had seen land to the southwest. Once again the men waited tensely for daylight. And at dawn, once again, the horizon was as bare as ever.

"Was it really land that we saw?" Pedro asked Peralonso. It was a quiet moment during their watch, when the ship lay as calmly as a sleeping

A crewmember swigs water from a jug similar to those carried on Columbus's ships.

gull under the stars.

"It was land—land as real as the red earth of Pálos," Peralonso assured him.

"But if the admiral has a map that shows there is land ahead of us, why doesn't he tell us how far away it is?"

"These Genoese..." Peralonso spat into the water and fell silent.

They saw many birds. When the birds fluttered over the ship, Pedro and the other *grommets* staged contests to hit them with stones fired by slingshots. At sunset big flocks flew over, always heading toward the southwest.

"We should be looking for land in that direction," Peralonso Niño muttered. "It's obvious that the birds go there to spend the night."

But Columbus refused to change course, and he gave no reason.

Finally, twelve days after seeing the first island to the southwest, even Martín Alonso Pinzón lost

patience. On the evening of October 7, one of the largest flocks of birds they had seen passed over the fleet.

From his perch aloft, Pedro watched in disbelief as the *Pinta* swung around and began to follow them toward the southwest. Within just a few moments, the *Niña* did the same.

When he saw the caravels disobeying his orders, Columbus thumped the rail with his fist and his curses filled the air. But he could do nothing. The *Santa María* was the slowest ship. She could never overtake the other two.

"Follow the *Pinta*!" he snapped at the helmsman, and his cabin door slammed behind him.

The sailors grinned. Pedro fingered the tiny hawk's bell under his shirt and made the sign of the cross. Perhaps their prayers would finally be answered. Now they must find land.

Three days later, Pedro climbed down to the hold to fetch water for the cook. When he lifted the barrel cover, he could see that the drinking water was covered with scum and filled with tiny larvae. He closed his eyes and swallowed hard. How much worse would the water get before they saw the hills of home again?

Behind him, the men were clustered together in an angry knot.

"It has been thirty-one days now since we left the Canary Islands. We have voyaged farther than any man believed possible," they agreed.

The next morning, when the three ships came together as usual, the men shouted to each other that they would go no farther.

"The men are right," Martín Alonso shouted to Columbus. "It's time to turn back!"

Columbus stood silent. Finally he ordered, "Leave a few men in each ship. The rest of you, come aboard here."

Soon the main deck of the *Santa María* was filled with men huddled in groups, their eyes angry and determined. From the front of the poop deck,

Right: **When the sailors insist they will go no farther, Columbus explains that he has a secret map showing the route to the New World.**

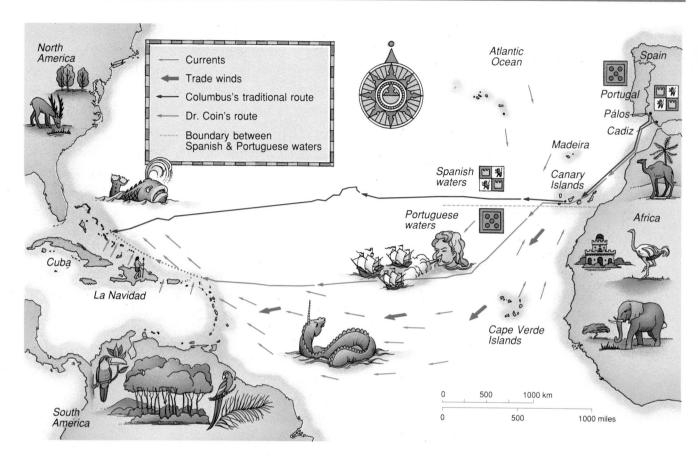

This map shows the route historians believe Columbus took from Spain to the New World and the route we followed based on Dr. Coin's theory that Columbus had a secret map. When they were close to the New World, Columbus and his men sighted land three times and then lost it because of currents that pushed them northwest past the islands each night.

the admiral surveyed the crew. He held a rolled-up chart in his hands.

"Men, we have come far and you have been good seamen," he said coolly. "But we must finish what we have started..."

"You have brought us on a voyage to hell," spat one. "You lied to the king and queen about the land. You have lied to us!"

"Throw the admiral to the sharks!" came a rasping shout from the back of the crowd. Pedro knew it was Bartolomeo.

"We don't want to die!" called another.

"We have fulfilled our duty!"

The sailors began to whistle and jeer, until Martín Alonso strode forward with his brothers and snapped, "Shut your traps and listen!"

"I want to tell you a true story," Columbus went on, as the men fell silent. "A few years ago I was living with my wife's brother on the island of Porto Santo near Madeira. One day a small boat was washed up on the beach.

"It carried a few Portuguese sailors whose ship had sunk beneath them. They were sick with fever and starving, and they died in my house. Before he died, the pilot told me how the ship had sailed from Guinea, bound for Portugal. But a huge storm drove it far to the west."

Every man was silent now. The only sound was the creaking of the ship as it rolled gently on the waves.

"There they found beautiful islands and much gold," Columbus continued. "For a year they explored a paradise before turning for home. And this..." The admiral unrolled the chart between his hands so everyone could see it. "...this is the chart the pilot made of the islands. This is why we sailed south into Portuguese waters before turning west. The chart shows the first land at a distance of 750 leagues from the Canary Islands, and that is just where we found it.

"We have already seen land and lost it. We are being slowed by these feeble winds. I know we are close to bigger islands, even a great mainland. That is why we must sail on!"

The men shook their heads unhappily.

"Our water is already black and sour," one complained. "Our bread is covered with green mold and alive with worms."

Columbus held up his hand. "Three more days," he said quietly. "Let us sail on for three days, and if we do not find land..." He paused, and the entire ship seemed to hold its breath. "...if we do not find land, you can do with me what you will."

Martín Alonso stepped forward before any of the men could speak. "It's a fair request," he said. "If we sail on for three more days, the king and queen cannot say we turned back like traitors."

"Three more days," Peralonso Niño agreed finally.

"And not a minute longer," Juan de la Cosa added firmly.

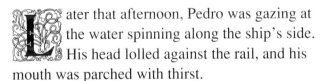 ater that afternoon, Pedro was gazing at the water spinning along the ship's side. His head lolled against the rail, and his mouth was parched with thirst.

Suddenly his half-closed eyes caught sight of something in the water. Quick as a flash he climbed outside the hull and snatched up a green stick as it floated past. It had long leaves, like a reed.

Excitedly he showed it to Peralonso Niño.

"Perhaps this time our prayers will be answered," the older man said. "That branch surely means that land is close."

The men stopped grumbling. Every pair of eyes searched the horizon ahead.

As the sun went down on the second day, the wind did not drop. The fleet was making good speed. With so little time left, Columbus decided to press on instead of slowing down during the night. The ships sailed hard through the darkness. The moon turned the sea to silver and gleamed on the pale sails of the caravels that were far ahead.

Then, at two o'clock in the morning on Friday, October 12, 1492, the soft sounds of the night were interrupted by the sudden crack of a gun being fired, the signal that land was in sight. Pedro jumped into the rigging and stared ahead.

There! Under the moon...! Was it a line of ghostly breakers bursting along a low rocky shore?

At once the sails were slackened and the

A crewmember fires the cannon when land is sighted, using bread rolls instead of cannon balls.

headlong dash of the three ships was halted.

Nobody slept as the little fleet waited for dawn. Throughout the night, Pedro prayed that this land, too, would not mysteriously vanish when the sun came up.

Slowly the moon set and the sky brightened in the east.

And slowly dawn's first light revealed land.

It was a flat green island ringed with white beaches. The emerald trees were thick with screeching birds. Pedro shouted out in astonishment when he saw human figures appear on the dazzling beach. They were naked men with black hair, their brown skins daubed with black, white and red paint.

With a cry of joy and relief, the boy kissed his hawk's bell and fell to his knees. Just as Columbus had promised, they had found a new world.

CHAPTER SIX

"THE SANTA MARÍA IS SINKING!"
Disaster in the Caribbean

We rowed to the shore of the New World *(top)* and planted a cross and gibbet in the sand, just as Columbus did *(above)*.

A s the anchor splashed down, the *Santa María*'s boat was hoisted over the side of the ship. The turquoise water was so clear that Pedro could see fish scattering when the anchor hit bottom. Quickly, he swarmed down a rope to claim his place at one of the oars. When it pushed off, the boat was so loaded with men that there was hardly room to row.

Christopher Columbus sat in the stern with his officials. All wore their finest clothes. The master-at-arms, his polished helmet and iron breastplate winking in the sun, stood in the front of the boat holding the flag of Castile.

"Steady there!" Pedro stopped rowing, and the boat crunched onto the sand. Pedro jumped out to hold it, the warm water swirling around his bare legs. The thud of solid land beneath his feet gave him a jolt that went all the way up his neck.

Sailors helped pull the boat farther in so Columbus and the officials could step ashore with dry feet. Nearby, the boats from the two caravels were also landing.

Dozens of natives watched from under the trees as the knot of men carrying banners and flags walked up the beach.

Columbus fell to his knees and uttered fervent thanks to God for delivering them safely. Pedro joined in the prayers, though he really just wanted to dance with the pleasure of feeling dry land beneath his toes.

A tall wooden cross and a gibbet with a hangman's noose dangling from it were planted upright at the top of the beach. In ringing tones the master-at-arms took possession of the island in the name of the queen of Castile.

"From this time," he declared, "the Christian faith, represented by this cross, and Castilian justice, represented by this gibbet, will rule over these new-found lands."

Out of the corner of his eye, Pedro watched a few of the natives tiptoe out of the shelter of the trees. Their dark eyes were round with astonishment. They carried fragile spears made of reed or wood and tipped with fish bone.

"Come, we mean you no harm!" Columbus called, beckoning with a smile. But the sound of his loud voice and strange words only made the natives run away.

Suddenly, Pedro noticed a slight movement in a bush just a few steps away. Half hidden behind it was a native boy, not much older than Pedro and naked except for stripes of red that smeared his forehead.

Pedro smiled and stepped forward. The boy stepped backward hastily. Pedro stopped, and the boy stopped.

Then Pedro had an idea. From inside his shirt he took out the little bell his mother had given him. Holding it between his thumb and forefinger, he made it ring. The boy's eyes gleamed. Pedro removed the bell from his neck and held it out.

Nervous as a bird, the boy stretched out his hand. With a quick movement he snatched the bell. But when Pedro simply grinned, the boy's worried face split into a wide smile.

Other natives began to emerge from the trees.

Columbus and his men take possession of the New World. The natives called the island Guanahaní, but Columbus renamed it San Salvador.

They laughed and nodded happily when Columbus gave them handfuls of bright beads. With wonder, they rapped their knuckles on the master-at-arms' shiny breastplate and stroked the buttons of the admiral's red doublet. In turn, Pedro could see Columbus carefully eyeing the small gold ornaments that many of the natives wore in their ears and noses.

Ringing the hawk's bell over and over in his ear, the native boy reached out with his other hand and touched Pedro's cheek. When his exploring fingers touched the dagger on his belt, Pedro removed it from its sheath. But before he could stop him, the boy had grabbed the dagger by the

blade. He sprang backward with a cry, blood spurting from the cut in his hand.

As the natives gathered around, gazing at the dagger as if it were magic, Pedro demonstrated its powers by carving a stick. Then the master-at-arms prompted gasps when he drew his long sword and slashed at palm fronds as if they were enemy soldiers.

That night, the heavy perfume of flowers drifted out to the *Santa María*. Natives swam out to the ship and swarmed over the deck. Pedro watched them in the moonlit darkness and felt as if he were in the middle of a strange dream.

Pedro wanted to stay on the island forever, but after three days Columbus gave orders to make sail. The fleet raised anchors and sailed toward the southwest. Almost at once the horizon was dotted with so many islands that Columbus could not decide which one to visit first.

For the next two months Pedro felt as if he was in paradise. By day the ships sailed in calm seas

We recreate the ceremony performed by Columbus and his men, claiming the island for the queen.

from one beautiful island to the next. By night they rested in peaceful anchorages and the men rowed ashore to sparkling beaches. Wherever they landed, the native people who ran to greet them thought Columbus and his sailors were men from the sky.

Yet the admiral was restless, always anxious to push on to find the source of gold. He kept hearing about islands where people could gather gold on the beach and hammer it into bars, and about a mountainous area nearby that was filled with the precious metal.

But Pedro didn't care about gold. After weeks of foul water, beans and wormy bread, he just wanted to explore and swim and feast forever on the fresh fish and strange succulent fruits. Netting in the shallows, the men bagged hundreds of bright blue, yellow and red fish in a single haul. Pedro thought they looked like swimming parrots. He and the men grilled them on sticks over a fire, then washed their sticky fingers in the sea.

Every day he seemed to discover a creature he had never seen before. At one moonlit beach he saw turtles crawling ashore like lumbering rocks and depositing heaps of eggs in holes they had scooped out of the sand. Near another he saw huge creatures grazing on seaweed in the water. From a distance they looked almost human in shape. Pedro thought at first that they were the mermaids the sailors had told him about, but they were manatees. And along the marshy shore of a lake he found himself face to face with the ugliest creature he had ever seen. It looked like a small dragon. Suddenly it reared up on its hind legs. A cape of scaly skin spread out behind its head, and it glared at Pedro with angry red eyes.

Pedro stood frozen as he waited for the awful creature to breathe fire. Instead, it turned and scuttled into the undergrowth.

The fleet soon came to the coast of a large

The Spaniards searched for pieces of gold such as this one *(above)* in streams and river beds.

mountainous land that the natives called "Cuba." It was high and handsome country, quite different from the many small flat islands they had visited. The ships pulled into a deep, clear river mouth, its banks overhung with palms. At the hope of finding gold in the hills, Columbus's eyes took on a new gleam, and the frown on his face disappeared.

Along the shore, smoke rose from fires where natives were burning vegetation to make space for planting crops. The village was larger than the ones the Spaniards had seen before, with houses that had high peaked roofs like tents. As the ships' boats were rowed ashore, the natives didn't come out to greet them, but fled into the bushes.

The men swarmed over the village, poking their heads into the abandoned houses, examining baskets and tools. Pedro walked into one thatched hut at the edge of the village. The house was cool and comfortable, and the floor was covered with baskets filled with strange knobbly yellow vegetables wrapped in green leaves. He picked one up.

"*Maiz*," said a voice behind him. Pedro jumped and the vegetable fell out of his hand, dropping to the earthen floor with a dull thud. An old man stood in the doorway. He was sturdily built, with a wide face and high cheekbones, his skin tough and leathery from the sun. The man's expression was blank, unsmiling.

Pedro backed up a few steps. He bowed and smiled nervously, feeling like a robber who had been caught in someone's house.

The man went over to one of the baskets and grabbed a handful of dried leaves.

"*Tabacas*," he said. With a nod he beckoned Pedro to follow him outside where a small fire was burning. The boy watched as the man deftly rolled the leaves into a thin cylinder, then lit one end with a firebrand.

Dragons Of The New World

The drawing *(below)* is of an iguana, a kind of lizard found in the New World. Columbus's men soon discovered that the lizard's flesh was good to eat.

A native smokes tobacco leaves. This practice would soon spread throughout the world.

As Pedro looked on in amazement, the man placed the other end in one of his nostrils and loudly sniffed in the smoke. Then he took the cylinder out of his nose and handed it to the boy.

Pedro looked at the man's expressionless face and gulped. Then he put the end of the roll of burning leaves up his nose and breathed in the fragrant smoke.

Immediately he felt as if the inside of his head were on fire. His eyes teared up and he gagged on the smoke in a fit of coughing. The native man broke into a smile for the first time.

In the days that followed, Pedro learned a lot from his new friend. He gave the man a button from his shirt in exchange for a *hamaca*, a bed made of woven string, like a fishing net, and suspended between two poles or trees. That night, Pedro slung his new bed between two deck beams on the ship. As the ship rolled, the bed moved gently from side to side. It was the best night's sleep he had ever had on board. No longer would he have to worry about rolling into a pool of sticky tar in the middle of the night.

The next day, Pedro took Peralonso Niño to the native's hut. They sat in a small circle with the old man and two other villagers. The Spaniards

Right: **Pedro offers his new friend a button from his shirt in exchange for a *hamaca*.**

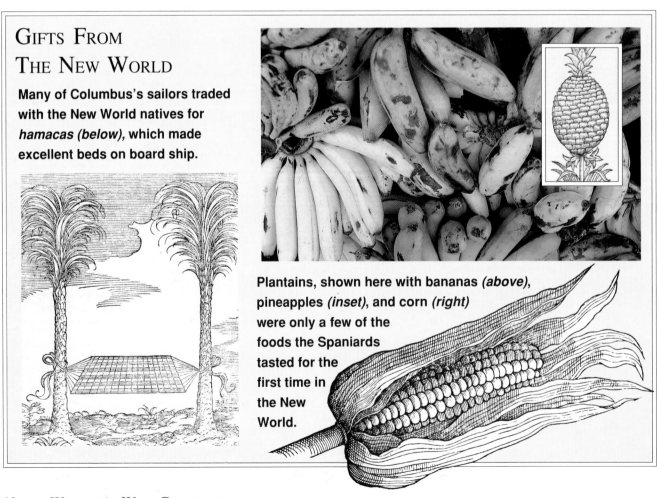

GIFTS FROM THE NEW WORLD

Many of Columbus's sailors traded with the New World natives for *hamacas (below)*, which made excellent beds on board ship.

Plantains, shown here with bananas *(above)*, pineapples *(inset)*, and corn *(right)* were only a few of the foods the Spaniards tasted for the first time in the New World.

had brought a bag of broken cups and dishes to trade with the natives for the gold ornaments that they wore. They were all so busy gesturing and smoking and laughing that they didn't notice the two tall shadows standing in the doorway. It was Columbus and Martín Alonso Pinzón.

Pedro couldn't hide his astonishment at seeing Columbus. Since their first landing, the admiral had not once stepped off the *Santa María*.

"All the gold belongs to the queen," Columbus said angrily. His ruddy face was even redder than usual.

Peralonso Niño stood up quickly, and buttons and bits of broken dishes tumbled from his lap to the floor.

"But you promised us we would all get rich, admiral," he protested.

"There's no harm in the men taking small ornaments, admiral," Martín Alonso said. "After all, it's the least they deserve—"

"I'll cut off the ears of any man who dares to take any gold for himself," Columbus threatened. And he stomped back to the beach.

The hope of finding gold objects such as this mask brought hundreds of Spanish adventurers to the New World.

For many days the fleet cruised the north coast of Cuba. All the men knew Columbus was feverishly looking for the big source of gold that he was convinced lay nearby. He no longer talked of finding new lands to claim for Castile. Instead he talked only of gold.

Finally, after several days of wearily zigzagging back and forth along the coast in teeming rains and contrary winds, Martín Alonso once again took matters into his own hands. One evening, instead of following the other two ships to shore, he turned the *Pinta* away from the fleet and sailed into the twilight. At dawn the next day

the caravel was nowhere in sight. Columbus was furious, but there was nothing he could do. Instead the *Santa María* and the *Niña* carried on to the east, beyond Cuba to another large island that he called La Española.

A few days before Christmas, the two ships were at anchor in a large bay when Pedro noticed a long and lean native canoe cutting toward them. It carried two native visitors with a gift for the admiral—a fabulous belt made of white fish bones, pure and lustrous as pearls, bound with tiny knots of cotton. Attached to the belt was a mask, its nose, mouth and two large ears made of pure hammered gold.

Columbus went almost mad with excitement when he saw it. He could almost smell the gold, Pedro knew.

The belt had been sent by a great chief who lived in a town along the coast. The *Santa María* and *Niña* immediately set sail to go there.

Christmas Eve was hot and bright. The wind blew first from one direction, then another. When night fell, Columbus ordered Juan de la Cosa not to stop to anchor.

"The admiral is being foolish," Pedro heard Peralonso Niño mutter. "It is dangerous to sail an unknown coast in darkness, no matter how light the winds."

As darkness settled, the *Santa María* fell silent. Pedro knew that the men were exhausted. It wasn't long before he, too, dozed off on deck, too tired even to hang his *hamaca*.

He was rudely wakened a short while later by the hard jab of a boot.

"You there, boy!" a harsh voice said. "Get up." It was Bartolomeo.

"But it's not my watch!" Pedro grumbled half to himself.

"Shut up," the Pálos murderer said roughly. "The admiral has put me in charge of steering, and now I'm giving the task to you. Do as you're told or I'll tickle your ribs with the point of my knife."

Pedro knew better than to argue with the glint of steel in Bartolomeo's hand. Reluctantly he took the tiller, then watched in dismay as the man plunked himself down on the deck, his back propped against the bulwark. Within a few moments his head had fallen forward with a gentle snore.

Pedro tried not to panic at the thought that he was the only one awake on the whole ship. He knew that no boy was ever to be left alone on watch. He gripped the smooth shaft of the tiller between his hands and fixed his eyes on the candle-lit steering compass. He moved the tiller first one way, then the other, and saw the compass needle swing from side to side. He began to relax. The *Santa María* barely moved through the water.

Looking forward, Pedro could see the full

Carlos takes the tiller *(inset)* as darkness falls over the *Niña*.

length of the maindeck and a little of the sea on either side. But the way straight ahead was hidden behind the high forecastle in the front of the ship. Pedro knew the lookouts atop the mast were probably dozing, too, but he wasn't worried. He might only be a ship's boy, but he had seen this done thousands of times.

Pedro concentrated on keeping the ship pointed southeast by east. The other boys would never believe he had steered the ship by himself through the night. Perhaps the admiral would be so impressed that he would make him a seaman. How proud his mother would be when he got home and told her about—

There was a strange feeling in the tiller. A vibration. The tiller wouldn't move! At the same moment, the deck tilted beneath Pedro's feet. The whole ship shivered, and a wave broke alongside with a smother of foam.

With a horrible feeling, Pedro realized what had happened. The terror in his throat was so thick that it was several seconds before he could shout out the dreadful words.

"Help! Captain, Captain! Help! The ship's on a rock!"

Overleaf: **The natives help Columbus and his men strip the shipwrecked *Santa María*.**

"THE *SANTA MARÍA* IS SINKING!"   51

CHAPTER SEVEN

THE *NIÑA* TO THE RESCUE

From disaster to triumph

Top: Steering in heavy seas, a crewmember throws his whole weight on the tiller.
Above: The *Niña* at dusk.

The *Santa María* had sailed headlong into a reef—an underwater ledge of sharp coral. Now, as every wave slapped into the ship's stern and pushed her farther up onto the reef, her timbers groaned and cracked and the sails thundered overhead.

Christopher Columbus was first on deck. With one glance he took in the pale and frightened face of Pedro heaving at the jammed tiller. He saw the sleeping sailors starting guiltily awake and the hissing wall of foam seething around the tilting hull. Beneath his feet the deck jarred and shivered. The *Santa María* was breaking up.

"Man the boat and lay out an anchor!" he shouted. "Let fly the sails! Empty the water casks!"

The men jumped to obey. They knew their lives depended

on fast action. The sails were lowered so the wind did not push the ship into more trouble. Everything heavy was flung over the side. The cannons were rolled over the rail with a splash. The casks of water and wine were smashed with axes to empty them. The rigging was cut through and the masts toppled overboard like falling trees.

But the sea was dropping with the tide. There was no longer enough water for the *Santa María* to float. Every wave lifted her up, then smashed her down on the reef. By the time the *Niña*'s boat arrived to help, it was too late. Lumps of coral had punched into the *Santa María*'s hull. Planks splintered and the ribs cracked. Water poured in.

At dawn on Christmas morning, the ship was lying nearly on her side, half filled with water and surrounded by floating wreckage.

Native canoes appeared from the island to help the men rescue what they could. Then the shipwrecked mariners followed them to a beach of white sand.

The boats and canoes nosed into a small river that twisted sharply to the left. There, on its muddy bank, they were welcomed by hundreds of natives and their chief who had sent the gold mask. Willing helpers carried the crew's possessions to a thatched hut, and the chief posted guards to protect them.

All day the boats and canoes paddled back and forth as the wreck was stripped of everything useful. Even the sails and some of the ship's timbers were brought ashore. Pedro rowed his boat until his arms ached, oddly grateful for the backbreaking work that at least kept his growing panic at bay.

He knew that the admiral didn't blame him for running the ship aground. As he had rowed one load of goods to shore, Columbus himself had helped Pedro unload them.

But how would they all sail home to Spain now? They would never be able to squeeze the flagship's crew of forty onto the little *Niña*.

Columbus decided to leave forty men on the island while the others sailed back to Spain to fetch more men and ships.

On the sand spit at the river's mouth, the Spaniards began to build a fort to live in. Because it was Christmas, Columbus called it *La Villa de*

Columbus called the natives "Indians" because he thought he had arrived at an island on the edge of Asia then called the Indies.

Navidad—the town of the Holy Birth.

Pedro wished he could stay. He was not looking forward to the trip home—a voyage that promised to be hard and cold when they fought the winter winds to the north. But no boys were chosen to remain on the island. Instead, he helped to stock the caravel with water, fruit and vegetables. Six natives who had been captured were chained together in the hold, along with other prizes of their voyage.

At sunrise on January 4, 1493, the *Niña* set sail for Spain.

The little caravel was less roomy than the

The new *Niña* battles fierce winds and heavy seas during the voyage.

Santa María but much faster. She had no "top" high on her mast from which to look out, so Pedro stood in the bow. It was there, on the first afternoon at sea, that he saw another sail.

"It's the *Pinta*!" he shouted.

The two caravels ran for an anchorage, and Martín Alonso Pinzón came aboard. Columbus greeted him in a rage. Through the thin walls of the admiral's cabin, the whole crew could hear every word.

Columbus told the *Pinta*'s captain that he had left the forty men behind.

"They will die and their blood will be on your hands!" Martín Alonso stormed. "In Spain you will answer for it. I will make sure of that."

"Oh, that we were in Spain!" retorted Columbus. "Then I would hang you from the door of your own house for the traitor you are!"

"The admiral's a fool," Juan de la Cosa said angrily, as he listened to the argument. "The *Pinta*'s navigator just told me that Martín Alonso journeyed inland on his own and found much gold. If we had followed him instead of Columbus, the *Santa María* would still be in one piece, and the

other men would not have been left behind."

Silently, Pedro began to be glad that he had not been chosen to stay at the fort.

n Wednesday, January 16, the last islands of the New World were lost from sight. Pedro could hardly believe it. The two caravels were finally setting their course for home!

But within days the warm skies and blue seas became a sailor's nightmare as the little *Niña* crashed over big green waves with spray flying along her deck. The days grew shorter and the nights colder as she drove to the northeast. When he wasn't on watch, Pedro hugged himself into a ball in his *hamaca*. In a corner of the hold, the six natives huddled together miserably.

After four weeks at sea, the two ships were hit by a tempest. The wind howled like a dog. The sky was an angry gray, the giant waves almost black and streaked with white. Often the crests broke over the rail and cascaded knee-deep along the deck. With no sail up, the *Niña* blew like a dry leaf before the wind. The *Pinta* was lost from sight.

Pedro's eyes were red from the salt and hollow with fatigue. As he clung to the rail, he almost prayed to God to let him die.

n March 15, two months after leaving the sparkling beaches and warm breezes of the New World, Pedro stood at the rail of the *Niña* as the battered little caravel caught the ingoing tide at the mouth of the River Tinto. His eyes filled as the spire of the church at Pálos came into view. He had long stopped hoping that he would ever see this sight again. Then looking back toward the sea he spotted a familar sail. The *Pinta* had survived the voyage after all!

The whole town stood on the foreshore as Columbus climbed down into the boat and Pedro leaned into the oars to row the admiral to shore. Would it be for the last time, the boy wondered.

He was no longer the lad who had sailed away in the *Santa María* eight months before. His hair was long and lank and stiff with salt, his skin darkened by ocean winds and tropical sun.

Now, home at last, the whole voyage hardly seemed real—the native huts, sea turtles and strange fruits were a distant dream. When the people of Pálos exclaimed at the brilliant parrots, fish bone spears and iguana skins the sailors had brought back, Pedro almost felt as if he were seeing them for the first time, too.

Then there was one last trip to make from the *Niña*—one last load of cargo. Pedro rowed the

Columbus presents himself in triumph to the queen and king on his return to Spain.

boat back to the ship and the four natives who had survived the voyage climbed down from the deck in shackles. As one of them stumbled to gain a foothold in the boat, Pedro reached out and grabbed the man's arm to help him, and their eyes locked for an instant. But the young native wrenched his arm away, his eyes flashing bitter resentment.

That night, Pedro lay awake listening to the soft sounds that the goats, sheep and mules made in their stable. His mother smiled in her sleep, happy to have her only son at home again.

But Pedro fidgeted on his straw mattress. He couldn't sleep. The bed was too flat, too hard, too still.

Suddenly he had an idea. And only ten minutes later, the young ship's boy had fallen into a deep slumber. His *hamaca*, slung from the rafters of the stable, swung gently as he snored.

SAILING WITH COLUMBUS'S GHOST

The new Niña *finds the New World*

As our caravel *Niña* rolled and tossed during her third week across the Atlantic, it was hard for me to believe that nearly five centuries had passed since Christopher Columbus sailed this way.

For three weeks now we had lived like fifteenth-century seamen, sleeping on rough wooden planks sticky with black tar, washing our dirty clothes in buckets dropped over the side of the ship, and in rough weather half crawling along the deck from one slippery handhold to the next like chimpanzees.

We had had our share of laughs, adventures and near misses. When ten rabbits escaped from their cage and hopped crazily around the swaying deck, we chased them on our hands and knees. We

In mid-ocean *(above)* crewmembers lower the mainsail so the rigging can be checked.
***(Right)* The new *Niña* makes her way across the Atlantic under full sail.**

had been stuck in a flat calm that left the ship wallowing madly on the ocean. We had been horribly seasick. One of the men had been whipped over the side into the sea by a rope, but just managed to grab hold of it and claw his way to safety.

Day and night our *Niña* plowed a crooked furrow toward the sunset. Twelve days out, like Columbus, we caught a tuna. Tropic birds circled us miles from land, just as they had the *Santa María*. And, like Columbus, we saw a meteorite

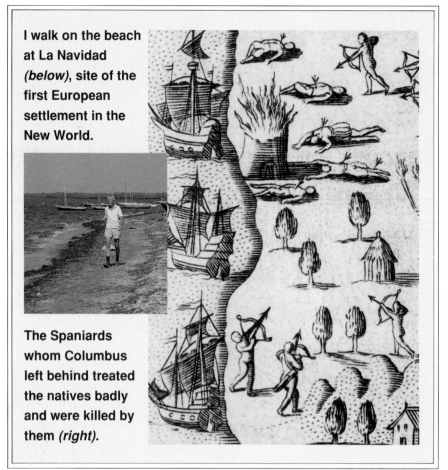

I walk on the beach at La Navidad *(below)*, site of the first European settlement in the New World.

The Spaniards whom Columbus left behind treated the natives badly and were killed by them *(right)*.

These men expected an easy life, but instead they lived miserably in a swamp. Finding gold was hard work, food crops failed, and many died of fever. The Spaniards believed the natives were to be ruled by the sword. And when the natives fought back, Columbus punished them.

More than one thousand natives were rounded up and five hundred of them were shipped to Spain to be sold as slaves. Columbus decreed that every native over fourteen years old had to produce a hawk's bell filled with gold dust every three months. Those who didn't were tortured, and if they fled, they were hunted down with dogs. Thousands of natives poisoned themselves to escape this reign of terror.

Soon almost every member of the gentle race of Taino Indians had been wiped out. The colonies were becoming so depleted of natives that the Spanish began shipping in slaves, first from Spain and then from Africa, to provide a work force. Over the next three hundred years millions of Africans would be uprooted from their homelands and brought captive to the New World.

On his third voyage across the Atlantic in 1498, Columbus stepped ashore on the southern mainland of what is now known as South America. By then Columbus had become ill and was almost blind. When he returned to the settlement in the islands he found many of the Spaniards stricken with fever, the others in revolt. In his weakened state, Columbus couldn't cope with the problems he faced as governor. In 1500 the monarchs ordered Columbus's arrest, and he was shipped home in chains. Stripped of his powers, Columbus became a pathetic and scorned figure.

Still Columbus petitioned the king and queen to commission a fourth voyage to the New World.

blaze overhead and explode in a shower of sparks. It almost seemed as if we had a ghost on board—the ghost of Christopher Columbus. I could easily imagine the tall figure of the admiral standing on the poop deck, his white hair streaming in the wind.

I thought of the amazing changes this man and his remarkable first voyage of 1492 had brought upon the world. Two parts of the world came together—the Old and the New—and neither was the same from Columbus's time on.

Six months after his triumphant return to Spain, Columbus sailed back to the New World in command of a fleet of seventeen ships. On this second voyage, he stopped at *La Villa de Navidad* only to find the grim remains of a massacre. The forty men he had left behind had been killed by the natives whom they had overworked and tortured.

Columbus had been made governor of the New World by the queen of Castile, but he could not control the Spaniards he had brought with him.

This voyage was also a failure: Columbus made no new discoveries, brought home no gold, lost his ships and returned in broken health.

When Christopher Columbus died in Spain in 1506, his passing was barely noticed. But thanks to him about 7,000 miles (11,200 kilometres) of coastline of the Americas had been explored. Columbus himself never understood the great extent and importance of his voyages. Twenty-five years later, the Spaniards reached Mexico and news of the great wealth of the natives there triggered the rampage of the conquistadores, ruthless soldiers who gave Spain control over

Columbus proved to be an incompetent governor of the New World and in 1500 was shipped home to Spain in chains *(top)*. **He died six years later** *(above)*.

huge areas of North America, much of South America and nearly all the Caribbean. Soon great treasure galleons were bringing to Spain four tons of gold every year.

In spite of his vision and courageous voyages, the New World was not named after Christopher Columbus. In 1504 an Italian called Amerigo Vespucci, who had himself sailed to the New World, took the information he had accumulated from Columbus's four voyages and passed it to a foreign mapmaker.

So it was not the name of Columbus that was engraved on the new lands, but America.

DID COLUMBUS HAVE A SECRET MAP?

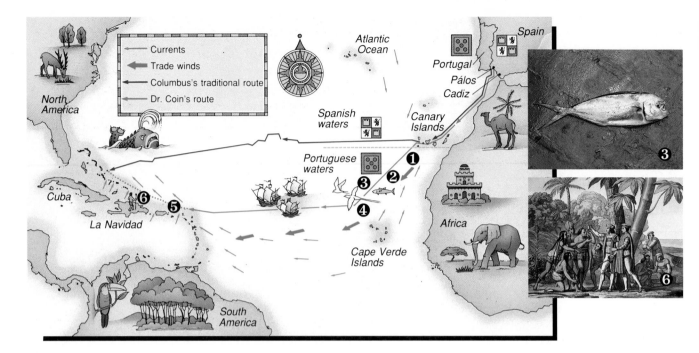

Currents
Trade winds
Columbus's traditional route
Dr. Coin's route

Atlantic Ocean

Spain

Portugal
Pálos
Cadiz

North America

Spanish waters

Canary Islands

Portuguese waters

Cuba

La Navidad

Africa

Cape Verde Islands

South America

Historians have always accepted the story Columbus tells in his journal of how he followed the setting sun west from the Canary Islands until he reached land.

But when Dr. Coin, an experienced sailor, read the journal, he realized that on many days Columbus described things he couldn't possibly have seen if he had really been sailing straight west. On the other hand, Columbus could easily have seen these things if he had first sailed south into Portuguese waters and then turned west. But why would he lie about his true route?

Dr. Coin believes that Columbus kept a true account of what he saw on each day of the voyage, and a false record of his location. That way, if he were captured by the enemy Portuguese, he could use his journal to "prove" that he had made his voyage in friendly Spanish waters. Columbus feared that if the Portuguese learned that he had trespassed in their zone they would execute him and claim the New World as their own.

The fact that Columbus was so determined to take this route south and then west—in spite of its many dangers—suggests that he was following not a dream, but a map given to him by someone who had sailed that way before him.

These are some of the clues Dr. Coin found in Columbus's journal:

❶ Columbus complains that the currents are flowing against him. Dr. Coin knew that if Columbus were where he claimed to be on this day, the currents should have carried his ships along easily.

❷ Columbus noted that the seawater was "less salty by half." On a course straight west, the sea never becomes less salty. But on the southward route, Columbus would have come to a place where a deep layer of fresh water rises to the surface of the ocean. Sailing south aboard the new *Niña* in 1990, we noticed in this area that the water we used to wash ourselves was less salty.

❸ Columbus's men catch a tuna. Almost five hundred years later, we also caught a tuna at the place where fresh water comes to the surface. These rich fishing grounds are not found west of the Canary Islands.

❹ Columbus is not surprised to see a tropic bird and a tern, two birds which he believed were never seen far from land. If he had really been sailing west, he would have been surprised to see these birds in mid-ocean. But on the southward route, he would have sailed within eighty miles of the Portuguese-controlled Cape Verde Islands, well within what he considered to be the range of these birds.

❺ On September 25 Columbus's men protest that they have sailed beyond the 750 leagues set out in their contracts and demand to go home. Then land is sighted, but lost again during the night, and Columbus struggles on for sixteen more days before he sets foot ashore. How would he have known in advance the exact distance to the first land if he were only following a hunch and had no map to guide him?

❻ Columbus offers the people of the New World simple beads and bells in exchange for gold. If he had really expected to reach highly developed countries like China and Japan as historians have always believed, why would Columbus have sailed with only ninety lightly armed sailors and a cargo of trinkets?

Both the traditional westward route of Columbus and Dr. Coin's newly reconstructed route, first south and then west, are based on Columbus's journal. The fact that two such different conclusions could have come from reading the same journal shows us that, even after five hundred years, a fresh mind can bring new interpretations to an old story.

GLOSSARY

aloft: In the rigging high above the deck.

anchorage: A safe place for ships to drop their anchors.

astern: Behind a ship.

bilge: The space inside the bottom of a ship where waste and water collect.

boatswain: The foreman and chief craftsman of a ship in charge of all repairs and work.

bow: The front end of a ship.

capstan: An upright barrel-shaped post mounted on the deck, made to revolve by the crew pushing on long bars. The capstan acts as a kind of winch for heavy hauling jobs such as raising the anchor.

caravel: A small, fast sailing vessel with two or three masts developed in Spain and Portugal in the fifteenth century for exploring the coast of Africa.

Christian: One who believes in the teachings of Jesus Christ.

compass: An instrument for determining directions by means of a magnetic needle that points to the north.

doublet: A close-fitting jacket worn by men in the fifteenth century.

ducat: A gold coin which was once used in a number of European countries.

edict: An order from the king or queen.

firebrand: A piece of burning wood.

flagship: The ship carrying the admiral of a fleet.

forecastle: A raised deck at the front of a ship.

foreshore: The narrow strip of beach or rocks beyond the reach of the waves.

galleon: A large, heavy Spanish sailing ship used to carry goods from Spain to the New World and back again.

gibbet: An upright post with a long arm attached used for hanging criminals.

grommet: A ship's boy.

hatch: An opening in the deck of the ship which allows access to the hold. The hatchway is the passage with a ladder leading down to the hold.

helmsman: The person who steers the ship.

hold: The area below the deck of a ship where the cargo is stored.

Jew: One of Hebrew descent; one whose religion is Judaism.

larvae: Insects newly hatched from their eggs which live in water.

league: A distance of 3.18 nautical miles (3.6 miles or 5.75 kilometres).

manacle: A handcuff.

manatee: An aquatic mammal which lives in tropical seas and looks like a large seal.

marina: A dock where boats can be tied.

mariner: A sailor.

mast: The long upright wooden pole on a ship's deck used to support the sails and the rigging. The mainmast is a ship's largest mast and is usually found in the middle of the ship.

master-at-arms: The chief police officer on a ship.

Muslim: One who believes in the Islamic faith, through the teachings of the prophet Muhammad.

navigation: Method of finding the way a ship could take along a coast or across an ocean.

poop deck: The high deck at the stern of a ship.

rigging: The ropes used to support and adjust the sails of a ship.

rudder: A broad, flat piece of wood, hinged to the stern of a ship, which is used for steering.

shackle: An early kind of handcuff.

sheath: A leather pouch for carrying a knife.

squall: A sudden gust of wind.

stern: The back of a ship.

tempest: A violent storm.

tiller: A wooden bar connected to the rudder which the helmsman turns from side to side to steer the ship.

trade winds: The winds which blow constantly across the Atlantic Ocean from east to west.

wake: The track of foam and disturbed water that a moving ship leaves behind it.

wharf: A wooden or stone platform beside which a ship may be loaded or unloaded.

woodcut: A print made from a block of carved wood.

yard: A long wooden spar or pole, hoisted up the mast, to which the sail is attached.

yardarm: The end of a yard.

RECOMMENDED FURTHER READING

I, Columbus
*edited by Peter and Connie Roop/illustrated by
Peter E. Hanson–1990*
(Walker Publishing Company, Inc., U.S. / Thomas
Allen & Son, Canada, Limited)
Illustrated excerpts from Columbus's journals provide
a firsthand account of the 1492 voyage.

Columbus and the World Around Him
by Milton Meltzer–1990
(Franklin Watts Inc., U.S., U.K., Canada, Australia)
The story of Columbus's landing in America and its meaning
for the peoples of the Old and New Worlds.

Columbus: For Gold, God and Glory
by John Dyson/photographs by Peter Christopher–1991
(Simon & Schuster, U.S. / Hodder & Stoughton
Publishers, U.K. / Penguin Books, Canada)
This fascinating, fully illustrated account of the life of Christopher
Columbus sheds new light on his voyages to the New World
and tells the story of a 1990 recreation of his voyage aboard an
exact replica of the *Niña*.

The Discovery of the Americas
by Betsy Maestro/illustrated by Giulio Maestro–1991
(Lothrop, Lee & Shepard Books, U.S.)
Discoveries and explorations of the Americas are described
and fully illustrated.

John Dyson and **Peter Christopher** would like to express their
thanks to: The students and teaching staff of the Nautical College of
the University of Cadiz and Sr. José Luis Romero Palanco, Rector;
Captain Juan Landeta Bilbao and Captain José M. Spiegelberg,
director and assistant director of the Nautical College; The
Fundación Rafael Alberti, Diputación Provincial de Cadiz, owner of
the caravel; Barry Fox, chief executive of Fox Television Ltd. of
London and his crew Peter Fox and Roy Page; Captain Fernando
Benítez; Trasatlantica Line; Professor Juan M. Nieto Vales; Wm.
Harvey and Sons; CRAME of the Radio Holland Group; Dr. José-
Maria Luzon, director of the Archeological Museum of Madrid; Sr.
Humberto Ybarra Coello de Portugal of Hijos de Ybarra S.A.; Sr.
José-Tomás Carmona and Sr. Luis de Soto Ybarra of The Associa-
tion of Table Olive Exporters; Sr. Juan de Castellvi, Vice-President
of the Chamber of Commerce of Cadiz; Valeriano and José-Maria
Sanchez Sandoval and the workers of the Guadelete Boatyard in
Puerto de Santa Maria; Captain Rafael Lobeto, director-general of
the Merchant Marine of Spain; Porto Sherry Marina.

The crew of the *Niña* and her escort yacht *Tartessos* during the
Atlantic crossing, June-July 1990: José-Maria Anillo Muñoz,
Miguel Angel Blasco Molina, José-Luis Cano Manuel Diaz, Alvaro
Dusmet Garcia-Figueras, Antonio Gamera Aguirre, Gerardo Gantes
Rodriguez, Ambrosio Garcia Vara, Juan Lijó Pereles, David Lopez
Armario, Mata Majó Abella, Alfredo Martinez Vadillo, Luis
Fernando Morillo Montañes, Mariano Muñez Fernandez, Carlos
Platero Caraballo, Edouardo Presa Pereda, Pedro-Angel Puertas
Rios, Manuel Suero Alonso, Rafael Vides Sanches, Fernanda
Lazcano Pardo (doctor), Carlos Yañez-Barnuevo Garcia (doctor),
José Sevilla Gutierrez (cook), Juan Ignacio Liaño Ortuzar (cook),
Prof. Juan Mantero Betanzos (mate, *Tartessos*), Prof. Carlos Suavez
Escobar (captain, *Tartessos*), Dr. Luís Miguel Coin Cuenca
(captain, *Niña*).

PICTURE CREDITS

All photographs are by Peter Christopher
© 1990 unless otherwise stated.
Front cover: *(Middle inset) Le Llegada de
Colón a America.* Archivo Oronoz, Madrid
Back cover: *(Top)* Painting by Greg Ruhl
Poster: *(Left) Partida de Colón desde La
Rábida* by Cabral Bejarno. Arxiu MAS,
Barcelona
Endpapers: *La flotta di Colombo in rotta
per le Americhe* by Philopanos Honorius.
Giancarlo Costa, INDEX, Florence
Page 1: Museo Navale de Pegli, Genoa.
Fotoservice Fabri, INDEX
4-5: *Departure from Lisbon* by Theodor de
Bry. Giraudon/Art Resource
6-7: Painting by Ken Marschall
10: *(Top) La Caravelle di Colombo.* Fresco
in Villa de Albertis, Genoa. © Frederico
Arborio Mella, INDEX
12: *(Middle right)* Theodor de Bry. National
Maritime Museum, Greenwich
14: Archivo Oronoz
15: Painting by Greg Ruhl
16: *(Top left) Lectura de las Reales*

Pragmatica. Archivo Oronoz
(Bottom) Wesley Lowe
17: *(Left and right)* Details from *Virgen de
los Reyes Católicos* by Francisco Gallego.
Museo del Prado, Madrid, MAS
18: *(Top)* Museo Naval, Madrid, MAS
(Bottom) World map ca. 1489 by Henricus
Martellus Germanus. The Beinecke Rare
Book and Manuscript Library, Yale
University, New Haven *(Bottom inset)* Jack
McMaster/Margo Stahl
20: *(Top)* MAS
21: Painting by Ken Marschall
25: Painting by Greg Ruhl
28-29: Jack McMaster/Margo Stahl
32: *(Top) Odyssey* illustration. Archivo
Oronoz *(Bottom)* Bibliotheque Nationale,
Paris
35: Theodor de Bry. British Library
37: Painting by Greg Ruhl
38: *(Middle)* The Bettmann Archive
41: Painting by Greg Ruhl
42: Jack McMaster/Margo Stahl
45: *Landing of Columbus* by Cornelius
Vanderlyn. Library of Congress
47: *(Top)* Cynthia Brito/F4, D. Donne

Bryant Stock *(Bottom)* INDEX
48: *(Top)* Thévet, "Singularitez" British
Library *(Middle right)* © D. Donne Bryant
(Inset, bottom left and bottom right)
Woodcuts from Ramusio's *Navigationi
et Viaggi*, Venice, 1565. Giancarlo
Costa, INDEX
49: Painting by Greg Ruhl
50: © Adam Woolfitt, Susan Griggs Agency
52-53: Painting by Greg Ruhl
55: Studio Pizzi, INDEX
57: *Colombo é ricevuto dal Re Ferdinando
di Spagna al ritorno dal primo viaggio.*
Giancarlo Costa, INDEX
60: *(Right)* British Musem *(Inset)* Courtesy
John Dyson
61: *(Top) Columbus in chains* by Lorenzo
Delleari. Bridgeman Art Library *(Bottom)*
Archivo Oronoz
62: *(Top)* Jack McMaster/Margo Stahl
(Bottom right inset) Studio Pizzi, INDEX

Madison Press Books would like to thank
the following people for their assistance and
advice: Rick Archbold, Roger Barrable and
Sabine Oppenländer.